Miami
Gets It Straight

by Patricia & Fredrick McKissack
illustrated by Michael Chesworth

A STEPPING STONE BOOK™
Random House New York

For MaJon Carwell, Sarah Sade Davis,
and John Fitzpatrick McKissack
—P.M. & F.M.

To Lucy
—M.C.

Text copyright © 2000 by Patricia C. McKissack and Fredrick L. McKissack, Sr.
Illustrations copyright © 2000 by Random House, Inc. All rights reserved under
International and Pan-American Copyright Conventions. Published in the
United States by Random House Children's Books, a division of Random House,
Inc., New York, and simultaneously in Canada by Random House of Canada
Limited, Toronto. Originally published by Golden Books, an imprint of Random
House Children's Books, a division of Random House, Inc., New York, in 2000.

www.randomhouse.com/kids

Library of Congress Cataloging-in-Publication Data
McKissack, Pat.
Miami gets it straight / by Patricia & Fredrick McKissack ; illustrated by
Michael Chesworth. — 1st Random House ed.
    p.   cm.   (A Stepping Stone book)
SUMMARY: The school year is almost over, but nine-year-old Miami still has to
deal with his nemesis, Destinee Tate, and also faces a challenge when he shops
for a gift for his teacher.
ISBN 0-307-26501-3 (pbk.) — ISBN 0-307-46501-2 (lib. bdg.)
[1. Schools—Fiction. 2. Gifts—Fiction. 3. African Americans—Fiction.]
I. McKissack, Fredrick. II. Chesworth, Michael, ill. III. Title. IV. Series.
PZ7.M478693Mf 2004 [Fic]—dc22 2003017439

First Random House Edition
Printed in the United States of America   13 12 11 10 9 8 7 6 5 4

RANDOM HOUSE and colophon are registered trademarks and A STEPPING STONE
BOOK and colophon are trademarks of Random House, Inc.

Contents

1
Hot, Hot to Summer

Monday, June 1, 7:02 A.M.

We're hot, hot to summer! Five more days 'til school's out! No more math homework. No more book reports. No more geography work sheets.

And no more big-mouthed girls. The ones who always got something to say. Like Destinee Tate. My main enemy.

This time next week, String and I will be on our way to sports camp at Camp Atwater. That's in Wisconsin. But for now, we've got to get through this week. First things first, as Daddy always says.

String is my partner. We've been knowing

each other since we hung out in strollers. We started school together. And we're both in Ms. Rollins's 3T class. For five more days, that is.

String's tall and skinny. Wears glasses and a major league baseball cap all the time. Backwards.

Next to him, I'm average. Not tall. Not short. Just a regular nine-year-old young brother on the move. We share most everything—books, games, homework. We even had a birthday party together.

I racked up $25 in gift money on my last birthday. Check this out. Mama says I get to spend it on anything I want! I'm getting cool stuff for camp.

String plucks a hot waffle out of the toaster and drowns it in syrup. "May I have the rest of your banana?" he asks.

"Sure."

He cuts it up over his waffle. All the time I'm wondering where he'll put it.

String loves to eat. He talks about food. He sings about food. Food makes him dance.

In fact, he eats breakfast at his own house. Then he has a second breakfast at my house.

He should be huge. But instead, he's real skinny. So skinny, he can hide behind a shoestring. That's why everybody calls him String. Not by his real name, Christopher Tyler.

Nobody calls me by my real name either. Mama and Daddy named me Michael Andrew Jackson after my two grandfathers. When I was two years old, some people started calling me Mike Andy for short.

String thought they were saying Mi-a-mi. Miami Jackson. That's me. I like my name. I like my friend.

7:18 A.M.

String pours himself a glass of milk. My sister Leesie lowers the Missouri drivers training manual from in front of her face. "Don't they feed him at the zoo?" she asks.

Leesie talks to us with her nose turned up.

String's an only child, but I've taught him how to handle a big sister. He comes back quick with, "Think you'll pass your driver's test...on the third try?"

Slam! "Broke your face," I say. I'm laughing so hard I almost fall out of the chair.

Leesie glares at us. "I made a mistake

last time, okay? I didn't think they'd fail me for running just one little red light."

String and I are howling. Leesie tries for a rebound by saying, "When I do get my license, don't either one of you come asking me to drive you anywhere."

I'm ready with the block. "Why would we want to ride with *you?*" We're laughing even harder.

"Give your sister a break," Mama says as she comes into the kitchen. She's talking and walking in a hurry. "One more week of school! One more! No more early classes. I'm just not a morning person."

Mama teaches instrumental music at the junior college. Her specialty is the oboe. Most of the time she schedules her classes in the afternoon. Things go much smoother when she does.

"Hang tight, Mama," I say. "We're hot, hot, hot to summer."

Mama butters her toast. "What's that mean?"

I explain. "It's like when we play the game *Pin-the-flag-on-the-flagpole* during rainy-recess. I'm blindfolded. Ah-right? I'm holding the little flag with a thumbtack through it. I'm trying to find the paper so I can pin the flag on top of the little flag-pole."

I close my eyes and act out what I'm describing. "When I move away from the top, everybody yells, *cold, colder, ice-cold!* Got it, now?"

String leaps to his feet. He licks syrup off his fingers. "I know. I know. And when you move closer to the top, everybody yells *hot, hot, hot.*"

"Well, duh!" says Leesie.

All I do is pretend to be driving and that shuts her up with a quickness. She rolls her eyes and goes back to studying.

"Anyway, Mama," I go on, "we've got one week left before school's out. So, we're hot, hot to summer. Look out Camp Atwater."

String and I slap hands.

"Has anyone seen my keys?" Mama asks. "My glasses? Who's fed Shimmy and Shammy? Of all times for Mack to be out of town."

Daddy and Uncle Jay own a general contracting company—J-2 Engineering. Daddy's been away a lot this spring. They're working on a dam along the Mississippi River. I miss doing the Daddy things.

See, there's stuff I do with Mama. We watch sci-fi videos from the olden days.

Back when the monsters were dorky-looking.

Then there are things I do with Daddy. Like, he's into coin collecting. He takes me hiking. He's teaching me about both. I miss him.

But I've got baseball. That's my thing. I like coin collecting and sci-fi. But baseball is it. And at sports camp I'm going to play until I drop. Five more days.

I'm hot, hot to summer.

7:28 A.M.

String feeds our fish, Shimmy and Shammy. He's got a soft spot for animals. He likes taking care of them. People, too.

Mama finds her keys in her pocket. Her glasses are on her head. She's washing a vitamin pill down with grapefruit juice. She turns to Leesie and says, "I'll pick you up at three for the driver's test. Don't be nervous. Try to stay calm...."

Suddenly Leesie slams the book shut. "Mama! I wasn't even thinking nervous until you said the word!"

We laugh. Water fills Leesie's eyes. "You just wait," she screams at String and me. She grabs her backpack and rushes out the door in a huff. Mama steps to the side and lets all the drama slide past.

I've finally got Leesie figured. She's a homonym. Those are words that are spelled and said the same way. But they've got different meanings. Like a *strike* at a baseball game and a *strike* at the bowling alley. That's my sister. One minute she's Leesie-Laughing. In a heartbeat, she's Leesie-Crying. Spelled the same way, said the same way, Leesie is never the same. She's a walking, talking homonym.

Mama's leaving. She calls over her shoulder, "Give Leesie a break." She chuckles. "No pun intended." Mama likes to play with words, too.

She stops in her tracks. Sighs, then turns back to get her briefcase. It's still sitting on the counter. "What was that you said about being hot...?"

"Hot, hot to summer," I answer.

"Yes. Thank goodness we're hot, hot to summer." She throws us a kiss. Then she's gone.

Mrs. McCurtle wheels the big yellow school bus around the corner. String gulps the last swallow of milk. He tosses the banana peeling in the trash.

"Hurry up," I say. "We're hot, hot to late."

2
I Hate Destinee Tate

Same day, 8:28 A.M.

There goes Ms. Rollins, standing beside the door to Room 16. She's been greeting our third grade, Class T, the same way, every day, all year. And there go all the girls hanging around her. Sucking up. Especially the chief suck-up, Destinee Tate.

She's like the leader of the girls. A real bride of Dracula. I guess I'm sort of like the leader of the boys. The girls think the boys are all maggot brains. We're too cool for them, that's all!

Just five more days of Destinee Tate and

the rest of the girls in 3T. Then I don't have to see them all summer.

But I will miss Ms. Rollins.

Come Friday, Class T is heading for fourth grade. Ms. Rollins is leaving Turner Elementary.

She's heading for Ghana, West Africa. Going there to teach for two whole years.

Man, are those kids lucky. Ms. Rollins is a great teacher. And looking good, too!

We all hop in our seats just as the bell rings at eight-thirty.

"I hate Destinee Tate," I mumble under my breath.

String hears me. "You're still mad 'cause she won the spelling bee. You can't win everything, Miami!"

Destinee Tate is about the only thing we really disagree about. String likes her. I don't get it. He's friends with both of us.

I used to get mad at him for even talking to her. Made no difference. String will turn double-Dutch rope for the girls. Then he'll run over and hit a homer with the boys. He even sits with Rashetta Lewis—with her nose running all the time. Nasty. Gag!

String's okay like that. I understand. But I can't hang with Destinee Tate.

"You should get to know her," String is always saying.

"I know enough," is always my answer.

Ms. Rollins comes into the room. *The Star-Spangled Banner* crackles over the intercom. We stand. We sing. We say *The Pledge of Allegiance.*

That reminds me of Michael Keller. He made a big mistake last year. He started off the Pledge with the preamble to the

Constitution. "We the people..."

The girls aine never forgot it. They still call him We-the-People and fall out laughing. Poor Michael. I don't usually laugh at one of the boys in front of the girls, but that was funny.

Somebody hits my arm. It's Destinee. "We're having a meeting of the class officers at lunch," she whispers from two seats back. "Be there."

"Yeah, sure."

"Let's listen!" Ms. Rollins claps her hands.

"It was Miami," says Destinee.

Ferret-nose teacher's pet! Always got to be first. The best. The winner! Even if she has to cheat!

That's how Destinee Tate got to be class president. She cheated.

Here's what happened. There are fifteen girls and twelve boys in 3T. Destinee tells the girls to vote for her. She promises to make sure the girls get what they want!

There's another way to divide 3T. We've got sixteen kids of color. And eleven white kids. I could have asked all the black kids to vote for me simply because I'm black.

But I chose to run straight up. I told everybody to go with the best. That went over like two dead flies. I lost big time!

Well, not really. I'm the vice-president. Being vice-president is like beige wallpaper. Who notices? Who cares?

I wasn't the only boy to lose to a girl either. Destinee helped Amika take out Horace as class secretary. Lisa nudged David out of the treasurer's seat.

The only boy who got everybody's vote

was String. He's the sergeant at arms. Destinee, Amika, and Lisa are the majority. So they get everything their way.

If you say anything, they get all up in yo' face—bad breath, yellow teeth, and all. And whatever you do, don't make a mistake in front of the girls. They'll never, ever let you forget it. Just like poor We-the-People Michael Keller.

8:41 A.M.

Some fifth grader is reading the menu over the intercom. "For lunch, you will have a choice between a slice of vegetarian pizza. Or a sausage pizza. Buttered corn. Cinnamon applesauce. And chocolate pudding for dessert."

Everybody groans and starts to gag. Slop is slop—no matter what you call it.

I'm quiet. But I don't listen. I look at the bulletin board. There's a picture of Destinee right after she won the spelling bee. I missed the word *unanimous*. Too many n's.

It's not about losing the spelling bee. It's about all that studying, for what? To stand there trying to look cool while Destinee walked off with four tickets to a Cardinals baseball game. Destinee wouldn't know a baseball if it fell in her Cheerios.

The announcements end with the student reader giving the word for the day—"*compromise.*" The intercom crackles. It sputters and shuts off. And as always, every girl's hand shoots into the air. "Me, me, me, me," they whine.

We boys just sit with our arms folded. Waving our hands in the teacher's face is not cool.

Ms. Rollins looks around. "Destinee. You are our spelling bee champion this year. Spell the word for the day."

Man! I slide down in my seat. I don't want to hear all-a that.

Destinee bounces to her feet. I don't look at her. "That's an easy one," she says. She calls out the letters. "C-O-M-P-R-O-M-I-S-E. Compromise. Do you want me to tell you what it means?"

Show off!

"No," says Ms. Rollins. Her eyes move like radar around the room. "Miami. What do you think *compromise* means?"

Me? Ah-right! I stand up real slow, 'cause I'm thinking. "It's...it's a Jerome."

Destinee giggles. All the others girls do, too. I try not to pay any attention to them.

"It's like this. The Red Hawks wanted to

sign Jerome Streeter for $17 mil. Jerome asked for $20 mil. The Red Hawks came back with an offer of $18.5 mil. Jerome signed. That's a compromise. Right?"

Ms. Rollins nods. "Good," she says, smiling.

That shut Destinee's mouth! The girls got nothing on me.

"Compromise is a word that helps us resolve problems," says Ms. Rollins.

Why is she looking at me?

"One side gives a little and the other side gives a little. They go on like this until they reach an agreement that makes each side feel like a winner. Compromise. Make it your own word. Use it."

3
A Jerome

The morning zooms by and before I know it, it's lunch time. I'm chewing on a piece of veggie pizza with cardboard crust. Even String can't eat but one piece.

Here comes Destinee. Lisa and Amika are following. Their braids and beads are flipping and flopping from side to side. They remind me of Moe, Larry, and Curly.

As always, Destinee does the talking. The other two sock puppets do what she says.

"We think it would be a good idea to give Ms. Rollins a going-away gift. If everybody

22

in class puts in a dollar," Destinee says, adding in her head, "that comes to...to..."

"Twenty-seven dollars," I answer.

"I knew that," Destinee says, waving me off with her hand. "We've decided—"

"Wait a minute," I put in. "Who is *we?*"

"The class officers," Destinee answers, pointing to herself, Amika, and Lisa.

"What's your trouble?" says Lisa. "You should be happy we're telling you any-thing..."

"'Cause there are more of *us* than *you!*" Amika finishes. They slap hands. They know how to get to me. But I'm cool.

Destinee goes on with her plan. "It's Monday. We'll tell everybody today. We'll collect the money on Tuesday and Wed-nesday. Amika and I will buy the gift at the mall on Wednesday afternoon. Then Lisa will wrap it and get everybody to sign the card on Thursday. We'll give it to Ms. Rollins on Friday, the last day of school."

I hate Destinee Tate. Especially when she acts like she's president of the world.

"Why not have a party? Buy Ms. Rollins a big cake...have some punch and stuff?" says String.

Destinee gives him her chocolate pudding cup. "I don't think so," she says.

Course not. It wasn't her idea.

The girls act like they're all of that and a bag of potato chips, too. Ha! I'm tired of them bossing me—us—around.

"How come you and Amika get to pick out the gift?" I say.

"We have good taste," Amika answers.

I'm not backing down this time. "I have good taste!"

"Sure! Good taste in ugly." They all burst out laughing.

I do have good taste. Mama loved the glow-in-the-dark ballpoint pen I gave her for Mother's Day.

Even Leesie liked the fork and spoon earrings she got for her birthday. "Clip-ons!" she shouted. "They're so 1960."

I take a stand. "I can do a good job of picking a gift for Ms. Rollins."

Destinee folds her arms and narrows her beady blue eyes. She's not giving at all. "Not," she says. "What kind of wussy gift would you buy?"

"Order! Order!" String says. He finishes the last bit of chocolate pudding. "As the sergeant at arms, I say we need a Jerome." Then he turns to Amika. "Hey, may I have your orange?"

Amika shakes her head. "No way!" String shrugs.

Destinee lets a gush of air rush from her mouth. "Okay. Okay. Here it is."

Larry, Curly, and Moe go into a huddle. Moe—Destinee—turns to me and says, "What if we *all* go to the Crestwood Mall on Wednesday after school? We can pick out the gift together."

"All five of us?" I say. "Two is enough. What about String and me?"

"In your dreams." Then she folds her arms and stomps her foot. "It's you and me. And that's as good as it gets. What do you say?"

String gives me a thumbs up. The sock puppets each give Destinee a nod.

"Done."

Wow! A Jerome can work.

4
Sorry

Wednesday, June 3, 3:26 P.M.

Three days down. Two days to go. We're burning hot to summer!

Mama says our age difference won't matter when I'm thirty-two and Leesie is thirty-nine. There would be no problem now if we didn't have to share a bathroom.

Leesie finally passed her driver's test on Monday. She has been bouncing off the walls ever since.

She's in the bathroom now. On the phone. Talking to Marquisha. They're making plans for this afternoon. Mama is letting Leesie have the car. Leesie is going to be hard to live with after this.

But right now, I've got someplace to go. Destinee's mother is picking me up in about an hour to go to the mall.

Everything has worked out great so far. Everybody in class gave a dollar. We got Ms. Harper, the librarian, to hold the money for us. We raised $27. Enough to buy a nice gift. Then we all wrote down suggestions. Destinee and I will use the list to shop.

"Yo, Leesie! What's up with you so long in the bathroom?" I say. "You got a problem?"

"Gross! Go on with all that anyway," Leesie says, coming out at last. "My horoscope says I'm to be discovered today." She swishes down the hall. "So I have to be prepared."

The whole bathroom is steamy and smells like a flower shop. I'm not going in there.

"Discovered?" I shout. "Solar systems get discovered." I follow her down the hall. "Cures for diseases get discovered. Alyssa Jean Jackson is not a discovery."

She slams the door in my face. "What do you know, goofy?"

"Goofy! Who is it that dances with a poster of Denzel Washington? Then tell me again who's goofy."

The phone rings. She's got the cordless in her hand. But she lets it ring three times anyway.

"Hel-lo," she answers. Her voice changes from Leesie-the-Queen-of-Mean to Leesie-the-Princess-of-Sweetness. Just like that! I told you, she's a perfect homonym.

Suddenly, her door swings open. "For you!"

I look at the phone like it's a severed head.

"Take it!" She tosses it at me.

I catch it like a hot potato. It has to be a trick. Nobody ever calls me. String would come on over. We talked to Daddy this morning. Grandma calls on Sundays. So who is it?

"What's up?" I say. I'm not sure what to expect.

"Hey, Miami. It's me, Destinee Tate."

Gag me! Her voice sounds different. I've never heard her talk on the phone.

She's talking fast. "Something has happened. I can't go to the mall. You'll have to pick the gift by yourself. Come by my house to get the money."

"Me, come by your house?" I'm not ready for this. "Now? Today?" I'm thinking, what if somebody sees me?

"I can call Amika. She'll go pick the gift."

Hey, wait. I'm the vice-president. I'm supposed to take over in case the president can't do her duties. No matter what. "I'll be there," I say.

"Okay, then," she says, and hangs up without even saying good-bye.

Yes!

I let it all soak in. Destinee can't go to the mall! I start jumping up and down and all around. I'm going to pick Ms. Rollins a gift all by myself. Wow! Then something else comes to mind.

Daddy is out of town with his car. And Mama has promised to let Leesie use hers. How will I get to the mall? Too far to ride my bike. Man! This is seriously whacked!

3:45 P.M.

I go straight to Mama. She's at her desk fumbling with papers—the way she does when she doesn't want to work.

I tell her what's going on.

"I've got to go by Destinee Tate's house to get the money the class raised. Then I've got to buy Ms. Rollins a gift—all by my-self."

"All by yourself, huh? Big responsibility. How do you feel about that? Need help?"

"No way. I'm good to go," I say. "Except I need a ride to the mall."

Mama's eyes look like they're laughing. "Oh, I see," she says. "Hummm! Sorry. But the car is *Leesie's* all afternoon. You'll have to ask her."

"Ask me what?" Leesie comes bouncing into the den. She's in her show rags—pressed and dressed. Ready to be discovered.

I pretend I don't notice.

"Ask me what?" Leesie is real curious now.

Mama gives me a little nudge. "Miami has a favor to ask."

Mama is enjoying herself.

Here goes nothing. I decide to do a Band-Aid—say it fast. The way you yank a Band-Aid off. "I'm supposed to buy a going-away present for our teacher. Will you drive me to the mall?"

Leesie is like a block of ice. I wish she would say something—anything.

Finally the Frost Queen speaks. "If I take him and bring him back," she asks,

not even looking at me, "may I go out again?"

"Yes, providing it's not too late," Mama answers.

Leesie's got some serious drama on her face. She knows I'm at her mercy. But I'll beg if I have to.

"Okay," she says, looking right at me now. "I'll help you, but you've got to say you're sorry—sorry for giving me such a hard time about my driving."

Is that it? I mean, Leesie could have asked me for my whole allowance. She could have made me do her chores for a month. I would have done anything. "Hey! Done. I'm sorry. Let's go."

"No. No. No. Say you're sorry with more...more soul. Or stay home, Miami."

Mama can't hide the smile. She's pretending to read something.

I straighten up. "Leesie. I shouldn't have teased you about...when I said..."

You know how things get funny when they shouldn't? Like in church or when you're giving a report out loud? Well, the more I talk, the funnier it's getting to me.

"I'm sor...sor..." I burst out laughing.

Mama's shoulders are shaking. I know she's laughing. That makes me laugh harder. But I keep trying.

"Leesie! I really am...sor...sor...honest..."

"Just shut up, goofy," she says. Now I can see her trying hard not to laugh. But she chokes it down.

"Go wash your face," she says. "I can't be discovered with a dirtbag."

5
Friendship Is Priceless

Same day, 4:05 P.M.

In Leesie's mind, she's hauling me to the mall. In my mind, she's chauffeuring me. But first, we have to go by Destinee's house. She lives in Long Acres subdivision about four blocks from our house.

We find number 17. I'm out of the car like a flash. Before I can knock, the door swings open. Destinee is standing there on a crutch. Her ankle is bandaged.

"What did you do?"

She doesn't want to tell me. "I fell," she answers.

"Sorry."

"No, you're not!"

"Okay. If you say so."

"Here's the money." She shoves an envelope filled with dollar bills at me. "Don't you lose it, either. And you'd better buy something good—like what's on this list." She gives me a folded sheet of paper with gift suggestions the class has made.

Leesie blows the horn. I have to go.

"You coming to school tomorrow?" I ask, stuffing the money and the note in my coat pocket.

"If I have to crawl," Destinee answers.

4:46 P.M.

Leesie pulls into a parking space. Before we get out, she morphs into Leesie-the-Con-Artist. "Mama told me to stay with you," she says. "Help pick your teacher's

39

gift. But I could let you go on your own."

Leesie doesn't want to be bothered with me, really. That's fine. "Sure," I say, being very agreeable. "Go ahead. Mama doesn't need to know."

"You're gonna get to go a lot of places. Just keep that good attitude, little brother," says Leesie.

We go inside. It's crowded. "Make sure you meet me at the center fountain at six o'clock sharp," Leesie says. "That's when the little hand is on six, and the big hand is on twelve."

"A joke. Ha! Ha!" I say, walking away. She goes in the opposite direction.

I've got a bounce in my step. I've got money in both pockets. See, I've brought my birthday money along. Just in case I find a good deal.

It feels great. For once, the class president is not in charge. The vice-president is taking over.

First, I look over the list of gift suggestions the class made. Some of the ones I like are the pen set, a book, a sun hat, a sweatshirt, a pair of sunglasses, a set of earrings.

I wander through the bookstore. So many choices. Chocolates are always a nice gift. So are candles. None of those will impress the girls.

I look at a globe. I find Ghana in West Africa. Way to go, Ms. Rollins! She likes geography. But a globe doesn't do it for me. Not enough money anyway.

At the jewelry store, I find the perfect set of earrings. If I come back with these, that would sure blow the girls' minds. But the earrings cost over $70.

There's so much to see and smell in the mall. Time for a break.

5:11 P.M.

I come to my favorite place—Frison's Coin Shop. Daddy and I come here all the time. On the door there's a sign that says *Rare Egyptian Friendship Tokens*.

Man! I'm supposed to be shopping for Ms. Rollins. But I've got to go inside.

Mr. Frison is behind the counter. "Well, if it isn't my favorite customer, Miami. Come to see the tokens, I bet."

Mr. Frison explains that the tokens are copies of real ones. "They were found in a mummy's tomb."

Wow! He places one in my hand. Then he gives me a write-up about it: *Long ago, Egyptians gave these little tokens to special friends and family. The same way we send greeting cards to one another today.*

I rub the design. "That is a hieroglyph—a word picture—for friendship," Mr. Frison explains. "The hieroglyph on the other side means priceless. *Friendship is priceless.*"

Hey! I got to have this. It's a coin. It's about words. My thing. "How much?" I ask.

"For you, twenty-five dollars."

All my birthday money. That's ah-right. I'm going with it.

I pay for the coin. "Remember," Mr. Frison says, giving me the small bag, "these tokens should be given away to someone special."

Right. Outside the shop, I tuck the token in my jeans. I'm not giving this coin away. I can't wait to show Daddy.

Now if only I can find Ms. Rollins a gift.

6
A Good Deal

Still at the mall, 5:20 P.M.

Wow! Time is moving fast.

I'm standing at the Big Cookie counter when somebody says, "What's up?" I don't even have to look around. It's String.

"Hey, man. Where'd you come from?"

We high-five.

"My mom's getting her nails done. I came along. I was hoping I'd find you. You hear 'bout Destinee?"

He treats me to a juice. We split a cookie. We sit on a bench. "Yeah," I say. "She fell and hurt her ankle. Probably tripped over her long nose."

String bites into his half of the chocolate chip hazelnut cookie. He closes his eyes and listens to the taste. "Ummm. Did she tell you how she fell?" String asks.

"Who cares?" I say. "All I know is that she couldn't come. So I get to buy Ms. Rollins a gift by myself. Great, huh?"

"You need to know how Destinee hurt her ankle," String is saying, all the time slurping his drink.

"What, then?" I'm getting impatient.

"She was playing baseball, man!" String says. "And she hurt herself sliding into home plate."

Destinee Tate? Baseball? "When did she start playing baseball?"

String shrugged. "She just started playing this spring. She's learning. Getting good, though."

"Was she safe?"

"Scored the winning run."

No way, I'm thinking. The one thing I love to do—and what? Destinee Tate is trying to do it, too. "I hate that girl. You knew about this! And you didn't tell me? How can you stand her?" I ask without taking a breath.

"She asks me the same thing 'bout you all the time."

He goes back to munching on his cookie.

"Have you bought the gift yet?" Cookie crumbs fall out the side of his mouth.

"It's hard to find something the girls won't make fun of."

"Ms. Rollins like pretty things," he says.

"Whatever I choose, I want it to make those girls' eyes bug out."

String looks at me real funny. I wonder why.

Then I think of Destinee. "Hey, String?" I say.

"Yo."

"Did Destinee slide feet first? Or did she dive?"

String shrugs. "Randy was straddling the base. Destinee was rounding third. Denny threw long and high from center field. Destinee saw the ball and dove for home plate. Safe!"

Man!

5:33 P.M.

Hey! I got to go. Time is running out.

String can't shop with me. He has to meet his mother. I head for Bemiston's department store.

Who do I see coming down the escalators? Ms. Rollins with Mrs. O'Shay, one of the fourth-grade teachers. She'll probably be our teacher next year.

They are laughing and talking to each other. Acting like real people—not teachers at all.

Suddenly I get an idea. I duck behind a big potted plant. From there I can see Ms. Rollins shop. I'm thinking, that way I can get an idea of what she likes.

She goes to a perfume counter. She sniffs a couple of samples.

"This is the good stuff," she says. "The kind you can't buy on a teacher's salary." The two of them laugh. I like seeing them this way. They seem younger.

Next they go to the scarf counter. Ms. Rollins picks out a bright blue one.

"This would be nice with my white suit," she says. She ties it around her neck. "But the cloth is so beautiful in Ghana. I'll buy a scarf there."

"You must be so excited about your future," says Mrs. O'Shay.

"I am," says Ms. Rollins. "But I will never forget this year at Turner Elementary. It's been great."

Then Ms. Rollins moves to the handbag section. I have to move to the other side of the plant to keep from being seen. She stops at a display.

"Ohhh. This is a really nice package," says Ms. Rollins. She seems excited about it. So I pay attention.

"It has a diary, an address book, and a wallet, all three for one price," says Mrs. O'Shay.

"I would love to have something like this to take with me."

"Why don't you buy it?" asks Mrs. O'Shay.

"I sure like it, but there are so many other things I need more," says Ms. Rollins. And they move on.

I've found Ms. Rollins a gift! I make sure she is gone. I check the price. All three pieces come to $25. I have just enough.

Am I good or what?

7
Prince Creep

6:00 P.M.

I really got to go. I'm running out of time. I make it to the center fountain just as the six o'clock chimes are ringing.

Leesie and Marquisha are coming up the escalator to the main level. Even from a distance I can tell something is wrong.

There is a boy behind them. Looks like my sister's horoscope is right. She's been discovered—and, it seems, by a certified creep. He's leaning over and saying something to Leesie. Her eyes turn into lasers.

When they reach the top, Marquisha

splits. The Creep hangs on to Leesie. As they walk toward me, I get a good look at him. He's got some serious dreads and an earring in his ear. I can't hear, but Leesie's face is saying, "Leave me alone."

She comes closer. He follows. Then he grabs her shoulder. I've been warned not to speak to Leesie in public. But...

Suddenly, I'm possessed. I'm thinking I can jump in the face of a boy at least seven years older than me. He looks eight—no—ten feet tall. But there's no stopping me.

"Say, man. Why you got to be all over the lady like that?"

Caught him off guard. Leesie, too. She's standing there with her mouth hanging open.

The Creep looks at me hard. "What's

that I hear buzzing?" he asks. He eyes me up and down. "Oh! It's Mosquito Man!" He chuckles softly. "Watch out! Mosquitoes get...smacked."

He claps his hands shut. WHAM! The sound makes me jump.

I fall back into a fake karate stance. Like I'm a black belt or something. He steps forward. I do some fancy footwork and sidestep him.

All at once, Leesie moves in. Hands on her hips. "Touch my little brother, Amon, and it'll get real ugly."

"You heard her!" I pull myself tall. Trying hard not to look nine.

"Ohhh, so this is your brother. That explains..."

The Creep stands there stone still. His head is tilted to the side. The way Denzel

Washington holds his head.

To her surprise—and mine, too—he drops to one knee. He takes Leesie's hand in his.

Then coming straight out of Disney, he says, "I have offended you, my beautiful black princess. I am sincerely sorry. I beg your pardon."

He kisses the back of her hand. Then he turns to me, saying, "Is that cool with you, li'l bro?"

I'm figuring the guy for a real nut job. "Yeah. Yeah, man. Everything is cool." And we touch fists.

He winks at Leesie and walks away.

I can't believe the way she is looking at him. "Now that's how you say I'm sorry!" she whispers.

Okay, so he's Prince Creep.

6:12 P.M.

"You're not mad at me?" I ask on the way to the car.

"Mad? No. It is good for Amon to know I have a brother who has my back."

Now she winks. Smiles. Once again Leesie-the-Homonym!

We're on the way home. Leesie asks me to put in the new CD from Peace and Love. My heart stops! I don't have the brown and white Bemiston bag!

No gift! The diary, the address book, and the wallet are gone—missing.

"Think!" says Leesie. "When did you have it last?"

Everything is blank.

We hurry back inside the mall. I search all over the place. No bag. Nothing.

"It's not really lost." I refuse to believe

I've done something so stupid.

Leesie helps. She asks people passing by if they've seen a Bemiston bag. Nobody has.

We retrace my steps. No bag.

"Check with the lost and found!" Leesie says.

"Who ever turns anything in at the lost and found?" I'm angry and scared. I want to run. Hide. Fall in a hole. Disintegrate.

Leesie finally gets me to go home. I've lost Ms. Rollins's gift. I'm dead meat!

8
Saved!

7:40 P.M.

We get home. Mama is deep into grading papers. I beg Leesie not to tell what happened. She wants me to tell Mama, now.

"Mama told you to stay with me," I say. "But instead you went off to be discovered by the Creep."

"Stop," says Leesie. She grabs my arms. "Stop it, right now! You lost your own bag. Don't try to blame somebody else."

I pull away from her.

I'm really scared. Scared Mama might think I'm not ready to go to Camp Atwater.

Scared of how stupid I'm going to look. Scared of letting Ms. Rollins down. "Please, Leesie. Don't say anything to Mama yet. Give me time to think."

"Okay," she says to me. "We'll wait until morning."

7:55 P.M.

There's a box of fried chicken on the counter. The thought of eating makes me sick. "Hey there," Mama says. "What did you buy your teacher?"

"I don't want to talk about it," I say, and head straight to my room.

My room is another universe. And I am master of it.

The walls are painted space blue. When the lights are turned off, stars appear on the ceiling.

On one wall are my favorite sci-fi characters. Spock, Scotty, Captain Sisko, The Men in Black, and Ripley and the Alien. On the other wall are pictures of all my baseball heroes—Ken Griffey, Jr., Lou Brock, Hank Aaron, and Mark McGwire. Along with a poster of Satchel Paige, Cool Papa Bell, and Josh Gibson from the old Negro Leagues.

A mobile of the nine planets hangs from the light fixture. My NASA history timeline is over my bed, along with a poster of John Glenn.

I am happy in my room. It is a spaceship. In it I can go to the stars in a flash. I can find new planets and unknown galaxies.

The idea makes me feel like I'm riding a Ferris wheel.

Tonight I don't want to explore. I don't

want to find anything. I have messed up bad! And Destinee Tate is playing baseball.

What am I going to do? No gift. No money.

9:45 P.M.

That's it! I need money. If I had enough money I could buy another gift. But where...?

Slowly an idea comes. It's bad...awful... terrible. I can't make it go away. It grows quickly. Man! It makes me sick to even think about what I'm getting ready to do.

I slip out of my room. I walk down the hall to Mama's room. I go in. Her pocket-book is on the chest. She is downstairs grading papers. She always sticks money in the side pockets. I try to touch the pocket-book.

Stop! This is crazy. I run back to my room and hide my face. I am so ashamed.

Nothing is that important. I'll never go there again. I've got to think of a straight-up way to get out of this mess. Don't know how just yet.

10:12 P.M.

"Miami?"

I'm long past getting tucked in. But Mama still comes in to say good night. She used to read to me. Tell me stories. My favorites are about when she was a girl in Tennessee.

Now, we just talk. About anything, everything. Whatever.

Right now, I don't want to talk to Mama. I feel too ashamed, too sad.

I take long, slow breaths so she thinks

I'm asleep. Leesie taught me how to fake it.

Mama has a way of knowing when something isn't quite right. "Are you okay?" she asks.

No, I'm not okay, I'm thinking.

I've lost the teacher's gift. I'm ready to steal money from my mother. No, I'm not okay!

But I don't say a thing. I keep right on breathing slow and steady.

"Okay," she whispers. She's talking to me. But I'm supposed to be asleep. "Just two more days and school will be out. Daddy will be home. You can go to camp. Hang in there. We're hot, hot, and burning up to summer."

She starts out the door. Then she trips over my jeans.

She mumbles something and picks them

up. "What's this?" She finds the Egyptian coin I bought at the mall. "Ah," she says. "If I had bought this as a gift for *my* teacher, I'd be proud. This is a wonderful gift."

Mama shuts off the light as she leaves the room.

Yes! Yes! Yes! Mama thinks the coin is a good gift. So why not let it be the gift? Who would know? It costs the same as the other gift. And Mr. Frison says it should be given away. Perfect! Yes! Yes! Yes! I've been saved by an Egyptian friendship token.

I run to tell Leesie.

9
String Snaps

Thursday, June 4, 7:18 A.M.

String puts brown sugar on his oatmeal. I show him the friendship token.

"Wow," he says. "An old coin."

"No," I explain, "it's a friendship token." I remember what Mr. Frison said.

"It's like the ones they found in a mummy's tomb. The Egyptians gave these to friends like we send greeting cards."

"This gift is kicking," says String. "Ms. Rollins will love this."

"What do you think Destinee Tate will think?"

String gets this funny look on his face

like he did in the mall. He doesn't answer.

Then Mama smiles. "Miami, I'm so proud. It looks like you put a lot of thought into buying this gift. Your teacher will love knowing that it was picked especially for her."

I feel a little bit like a creep. Leesie glares at me over the top of the funny paper. She thinks I'm a jerk, too. But like I told her last night, hey, I'm desperate.

Mama looks at Leesie, then at me. She knows that Leesie knows something. Mama also knows that I know that she knows that Leesie knows something. But nobody's talking.

8:15 A.M.

We step off the bus. First thing, here comes Lisa and Amika. Destinee is limping behind them. They are all talking at once and acting excited.

Destinee asks, "What did you buy?"

We go to the library. I show them the Egyptian friendship token. "Egyptians used to give these to special friends and family," I explain.

"Oh, no," Amika screams. "You bought Ms. Rollins a grungy old coin! I knew it. I knew it. I knew you were going to mess up!"

Lisa looks at it. "You should have bought her something pretty like a scarf or a fancy pin. This is ugly. Just like you!"

"You aine seen ugly 'til you look in the mirror," I say. "That's ugly."

Destinee holds the token in her hand. It is her turn to hate it. "What was on your pea-sized brain when you bought this?"

"We should take this back. Get our money and buy another gift!" says Lisa.

"I wouldn't give this to a monkey," says Amika, shaking her head.

"I think Ms. Rollins will like it," says String.

Nobody hears him at first.

"You paid money for this?" Destinee says.

I bounce back hard. "It's a great gift, dummy."

"Who you calling dumb?" Destinee puts in.

"You, monkey breath."

We're all up in somebody's face, calling each other names.

Suddenly, String pounds his fist on the table. "Shut up! I'm sick of you, Destinee. I'm sick of you, too, Miami."

You can hear a pin drop.

"It aine about who bought the gift. It aine about who likes the gift. It's about Ms. Rollins. Is it right for her? That's what should matter. I think she'll like the coin."

String hasn't put that many words together in his life.

I'm expecting Destinee to go off. But she is really quiet—spooky quiet. What's on her mind? I'm wondering.

Then Destinee says, "Okay, let's vote on it. All in favor of giving the friendship token to Ms. Rollins, say aye."

Right away, I say aye.

"I say aye, too," says String.

Destinee thinks about it. Then she says, "I do, too. Aye."

Lisa and Amika are even more shocked than me. They stammer and mumble. But then they do what they always do—follow Destinee. "Okay. Aye," says Lisa, sock puppet number 1.

A second later, Amika, sock puppet number 2, whispers aye, too.

It is unanimous. We give Ms. Rollins the gift tomorrow. Unanimous. I've changed my mind. That's a good word, even though it cost me four tickets to see the Red Birds.

4:00 P.M.

String and I are sitting on the front steps, eating fresh strawberries and instant re-playing the day. He doesn't know it, but he has saved me from a fate worse than death. "If you hadn't told those girls off like you did, they would have never let us win."

String shakes his head. "You still don't get it, do you?"

"What?"

"It aine about none of that! The friendship token is a great gift. But you didn't buy it for Ms. Rollins."

"How did you know?" I say.

String looks surprised. "Know what?"

Uh-oh! He didn't know.

"I was talking about you buying the gift to please the girls," says String. "Okay. What really happened?"

I've never kept a secret from my partner before. So I tell String about the real gift, about losing it, almost thinking about stealing money from Mama, and finally getting the idea to give Ms. Rollins the friendship coin I'd really bought for myself. "Nobody knows the real truth but you," I say.

"What are you going to do?" String asks.

"Do? Nothing. Are you going to tell?"

String shakes his head. "No, I won't tell," he says, "but you can't make me like what you're doing. You're wrong for buying Ms. Rollins a gift just to impress the girls. And you're double wrong to give her a gift you didn't even buy for her. I can't hang with that!"

And for the first time, String goes home without finishing his snack.

I feel rotten inside. I wish to be beamed to another planet far away from here.

10
A Gift that Matters

Friday, June 5, 8:45 A.M.

The last day of school. This is it!

At Turner Elementary, everybody wears dress-up clothes on the last day of school. I don't know why. It makes no sense. We just do it.

String has been quiet all morning. Not much to say. I know he's mad at me. First thing, we meet with the girls. They vote that I be the one to give Ms. Rollins the gift after closing assembly.

"Since you bought the thing, you be the one to give it to her," says Lisa.

10:00 A.M.

At the closing assembly each class sits together. There is a review of the year. Ms. Rollins stopped letting String and me sit together after the first assembly in September. So, I'm sitting between Lisa and Amika. Ugh! Torture.

Mr. Hillshire blows into the microphone. The first graders giggle. Mr. Hillshire giggles, too.

Mr. Hillshire is the first and only principal Turner Elementary has ever had. As principals go, Mr. Hillshire is ah-right. I'm glad he's coming back next year.

He announces that we're getting a new fifth-grade teacher in the fall. Her name is Miss Amerita Spraggins. She's from Boston, Massachusetts. Wonder if she's been to Fenway Park?

Then Ms. Rollins and Mrs. Stone-Wilks are called to the stage. "These two teachers will not be returning next year," says Mr. Hillshire.

Mrs. Stone-Wilks is having a baby. Mr. Hillshire gives Mrs. Stone-Wilks a gift. It's a pretty yellow baby blanket. She holds it up for us to see. Her smile says she likes it. I'm hoping Ms. Rollins will smile when she sees the friendship token. But would she smile if she knew that I hadn't really bought it for her?

Next Mr. Hillshire makes a speech about how much Ms. Rollins will be missed next year. He gives her a present, too.

"Oh, this is too wonderful," she says.

Mrs. O'Shay steps to the microphone. "Boys and girls," she says, "Ms. Rollins picked her own gift." She explains, "We went shopping together."

I knew that.

"I watched what she admired," she says. "Ms. Rollins liked this. So, I hurried back to buy it the next evening."

Ms. Rollins holds up the box. It is just like the diary, wallet, and address book I bought...and lost!

I am too put out! All the girls ooh and ahh. The boys clap, stomp, and whistle. We can get away with that today only.

"Now that's the kind of gift you should have bought," Lisa whispers.

I can't stop laughing.

10:15 A.M.

We're back in class. My stomach is flip-flopping.

Destinee goes to the front of the class. "We have something for you, Ms. Rollins." Ms. Rollins smiles. "You have been a good teacher all year. We hope you like Africa. Please send e-mail to us. Okay?"

"Excuse me," says String. "I'd like to say something, too."

Oh, no, I'm thinking. He's going to spill his guts.

"I like getting gifts," he says. Somebody snickers. He keeps talking. "I also like to give gifts. I really hope you will enjoy this present as much as we enjoy giving it to you."

For the first time I realize what String has been trying to tell me. My feet feel glued to the floor. I make myself walk.

I know what I'd planned to say. But what I'm saying is not it.

"Ms. Rollins...I lost your gift."

Everybody laughs. They see the package in my hand. Destinee stares at me. "Stop being silly. Give it to her," she says through clenched teeth.

"Ms. Rollins," I say very softly, "I bought you a gift. Then I lost it. I bought this one, too. It's not the first gift. But I think it's the best gift. It's meant to be given to someone special. You are special. I want you to have it very much. We all do, really. We all hope you will like it."

"What's he saying?" Lisa asks.

"Something dumb again," says Amika.

Destinee is eyeballing me. Then she almost smiles. "Nothing. Nothing that's making any sense," she says.

Ms. Rollins doesn't seem to understand what I've said either. "Miami, you do have

a way with words." She opens the box.

Everybody is standing up, leaning forward so they can see. I'm all the time holding my breath. I can hear my heart beating.

"It is something we hope you will keep to remember us," I say.

Ms. Rollins looks at the Egyptian friendship token. She reads the little write-up. Then she bursts into tears.

"See!" shouts Lisa. "I knew she'd hate that ol' rusty thing."

"No, no," says Ms. Rollins. She holds up her hand. "I love this. I'm crying because I am so touched by your thoughtfulness. *Friendship is priceless*. This is such a treasure."

Everybody gathers around her to see the hieroglyphs on the coin. They are laughing and talking. I can breathe again.

Ms. Rollins looks at Destinee and me. "You were great class officers! You worked together so well all year. Let's give them a hand, for a job well done."

"Way to go, Miami," the boys cheer.

"Way to go, Destinee," the girls cheer.

"Way to go, partner," says String, smiling.

"We ah-right?" I say, holding up my hand.

String gives me a high five. "You did the right thing."

We've given Ms. Rollins a gift that makes her happy. And that is what really matters. I never want to buy another gift...ever, as long as I live.

3:00 P.M.

School's out. School's out. Everybody in

class passed to the fourth grade.

Off comes my coat. I pull my shirt out of my pants. I take off my socks. Oh yeah, school is out.

Me and String are on our way to Camp Atwater!

6:30 P.M.

Leesie's a senior now. Seems the homonym has a date with Prince Amon the Creep tonight.

We're celebrating, too! Mama has taken String and me out for pizza. Real pizza with good crust.

"Did Ms. Rollins like the friendship token?" Mama asks.

"She's going to put it on a chain. Every time she wears it, she'll remember 3T," I say, smiling.

Then I stop smiling.

Destinee Tate and her mother are coming in the door.

"Hello, Elise and Destinee," Mama says. "Come join us." Mama and Mrs. Tate work together at the junior college.

"Mama! Please," I whisper. But it's too late. They're coming over to our table. Mrs. Tate is almost dragging Destinee.

"I've been meaning to call you," says Mrs. Tate to Mama. "Destinee's won four tickets to tomorrow night's Cardinals game."

"I heard about that," Mama says, looking at me.

Mrs. Tate rushes on. "None of us can go except her dad. So would Miami and String like to go? I know they love baseball. Destinee's getting into the game herself."

"It's up to the boys," says Mama.

"Yeah! Sure! Thanks!" says String, taking another slice of pizza, his third.

Destinee's eyes are daring me to say yes.

I'm thinking, ordinarily I'd say no, but this is a Cardinals game and they're playing the Cubs. Man! I'd go with a grizzly bear if it had tickets.

"Sure. I mean, okay. Hey, thanks," I say.

Destinee folds her arms and leans back in the booth. "Well, Miami, you did come in *second* in the spelling bee. So in a way, I guess you deserve to go."

No way around it.

I hate Destinee Tate.

About the Authors

No one knows Miami Jackson better than Pat and Fred McKissack. After all, he came out of memories they have of their own kids growing up. "I took characteristics for Miami from all three of my sons," Pat says. "But Miami is a lot like my oldest, Fred Jr. He even had a tall, lanky friend like String." She also put a little bit of herself into *Miami Gets It Straight*. "I'm the mother," Pat admits. "I taught at the junior college. But I didn't play the oboe. I made that part up."

Pat McKissack is the author of many wonderful books for kids, including the Newbery Honor book *The Dark Thirty* and the Caldecott Honor book *Mirandy and Brother Wind*. Together she and her husband Fred wrote *Christmas in the Big House, Christmas in the Quarters*.